THE SURVIVORS

THE SURVIVORS

NICK FARMER

This book was designed by THE FRONTISPIECE. The text face is Minion Pro, designed by Robert Slimbach in 1990, with other elements set in RBN02 and Aldrich.

To all those who struggle to survive.

THE SURVIVORS

ONE

WHEN DANIEL WAS DROPPED OFF in front of his apartment building, he was beyond tired. It had been a long flight after a long trip, and he was feeling jet-lagged. He'd even splurged on a cab ride back to the city. His body was aching for a nap, but he had told himself he would try to stay up till a normal hour, to help himself adjust. Not for the first time, he was grateful to be in a building with an elevator.

He didn't really have anything else to do that day, so

he shuffled around his apartment, forcing himself to deal with the myriad of little domestic things that accumulate in life. He unpacked, watered the houseplants, and started to organize the mess on his desk. Yawning, he uncovered a stack of mail and flipped through it. Junk, junk, bill already paid online—but there at the bottom was a plain white envelope, with no return address. He hadn't yet gone to the post office for the hold mail, so it must have arrived before he had left on his trip. He'd missed it. Curiosity piqued, he sat down on his couch, opened the envelope, and started to read the handwritten letter it contained:

DANIEL,

IT'S UNCLE JEFF. I'M WRITING YOU BY SNAIL MAIL BECAUSE IT SEEMS LIKE EVERYTHING ELSE THESE DAYS IS MONITORED. IT'S EXTREMELY IMPORTANT THAT YOU COME TO MY HOUSE AS SOON AS POSSIBLE. DON'T CALL ME. DON'T TELL ANYONE YOU'RE SEEING ME, JUST GET INTO THE CAR, RIGHT NOW, AND COME.

There was more, but that was as far as Daniel got. He wouldn't even remember the bit that he'd read. Unable to resist the tug of exhaustion any longer, he tossed the letter on the coffee table, lay back for a nap, and fell asleep.

———————————

"Hey, Hoang, he's finally awake."

"The skeleton? You're kidding me. Damn, man, streak's over. I needed him to last for only two more days!"

"Actually, just one. You still lose."

Daniel opened his eyes. He was lying on his back, covered in blankets. "Wha—what?" he managed to get out. "Am I in the hospital? What happened?"

A young woman leaned over him, ignoring his question. She wasn't dressed like a doctor or nurse. In fact, she was wearing a black tank top under an open polyester hiking shirt, with hair tied back in a ponytail underneath a faded Yankees cap, but she pinched and prodded in a reassuring kind of way, like she knew what she was doing. Daniel tried to raise his head from the pillow, or even move it side to side, but he was overcome with weakness. Even keeping his eyes open felt like a strain. A man's face came into his field of view, features split into a huge grin.

"What's going on?" Daniel asked.

"Welcome to immortality, man!" he said. Daniel just looked at him, gave up trying to understand, and fell back asleep.

TWO

WHEN DANIEL WOKE AGAIN, he felt better—strong enough to even sit up. He was definitely in a hospital room, but he still had no idea how he had gotten there. The last he could remember, it was a muggy summer afternoon when he had lain down for a nap. Outside the small window, it looked like it was snowing now.

The woman who first woke him came into the room. "Oh, looks like you're awake for real now," she said. "You know, falling back asleep for a couple more days almost cost me my winnings. Don't worry though, I made Hoang pay up."

Daniel was full of questions, but all at once, his body reminded him he was empty of something else. "Um, I'm really hungry," he said.

"And I'm Esmy. Nice to meet you too."

"No, I mean—"

"Yeah, yeah, I know your name is actually Daniel. Got it off your ID. Anyways, here, I already brought you something to eat. Hope you like canned chili."

It wasn't his favorite, but at this point he didn't even care. He had no idea how long he'd been under, but from the look of his emaciated body and the snow outside, it must have been months. As he plowed through the canned food, Esmy sat down at the foot of the bed. When he finally slowed down enough to gasp out a question, he asked, "How long have I been out?"

"At least four months for sure, though probably longer. You were already here, half wasted away, when we moved in."

"When you…moved in? What do you mean moved in?" He finished the can and looked hopefully at Esmy to see whether she had more. She handed him another and continued.

"It seemed like a natural place to keep the sleepers. Lots of beds, IVs…you understand. We just took it over, got it running again. Sort of. Not many of us are doctors, not that that matters now, of course, but…"

Daniel shook his head. None of this was making sense. Had he hit his head—or had a stroke? Esmy, seeing his obvious confusion, asked, "Daniel, you must have been asleep a while. What's the last thing you remember before falling asleep?"

"Well, I was getting back to my apartment, cleaning things up. I had just gotten back from a conference in Europe."

Esmy looked shocked. "You were traveling? When was this? When did you fall asleep?"

"Well, it must have been—yeah, it was Sunday, June 24."

"June?" she said faintly. "That means…"

"Has anyone come to visit me?" he asked. "My uncle? Does my work know what happened to me? Actually, what *did* happen to me? You still haven't told me."

"If you got the virus that early, that means you were one of the very first. You...you slept through *all* of it."

"All of what?" he asked.

"The end of the world," she said.

Daniel chuckled. "Oh? So that idiot Miller got elected?"

"There never was an election. The government doesn't even exist anymore."

His laughter turned into a nervous giggle. Esmy looked dead serious. "What, so, the zombie apocalypse?" he joked. Or, well, he hoped it was a joke, but Esmy just nodded. "Sort of," she said. "Except, I guess you could say we're the zombies."

"You're kidding," he said, voice strained. "Right? Someone put you up to this. I was actually in a car accident or something, and I hit my head. I was in a coma." His breath came shallow, and he avoided her eyes. "Or I'm still in a coma. They say you see crazy things sometimes…"

Esmy sat down on the bed next to him and held his hand. After a while, when he had calmed down a little, she spoke again. "This isn't a prank, and you're as healthy as you've ever been. Healthier, in fact. It's a lot to process. Most everyone else who wakes up already has a bit of an idea of what has happened and is just happy to be alive. Things are different, yes, but it's not so bad. Come, see for yourself."

He finally looked at her again, and she smiled encouragingly. He took a deep breath and nodded. She had to help him get clothes on, and his first steps were unsure, but he quickly grew more steady. Soon he walked alongside Esmy without any assistance. Part of him knew that a man who'd lain in bed for months shouldn't be able to walk, but that was nothing compared to what he was being told. He didn't believe her, not really. It was impossible.

"Uh, is there more food?" he asked, as they ambled down the empty halls.

She rolled her eyes. "Armageddon, and some people still can only think with their stomachs." She eyed his bony frame and shrugged. "I guess, in your case, I can understand." She pulled some granola bars and a bottled water out of her backpack.

As Daniel munched away, he had a thought. "Is it safe for me to be eating so much? I mean, they say you can die if you eat too much after starving, right?"

"That's not something you need to worry about anymore," she replied. Daniel didn't know what to say to that, so he just kept eating. Winding down a set of stairs, they finally made it to the front door, which was propped open. They stepped outside, and Daniel let out a relieved sigh. Things looked normal. He recognized where he was, at the corner of 16th and First Ave. The city wasn't destroyed or vandalized, or littered with corpses and abandoned cars, like all the postapocalyptic movies and TV shows. Nevertheless, something was wrong.

"Where is everybody?" he asked. "It's so quiet."

"The few survivors are concentrated in Midtown. When the virus hit, nearly everyone fled the city, and most of the rest…most just died."

"How many?" he asked.

"We have no way of knowing for sure. Too many to count, but as far as we can tell, fewer than one in a thousand survive infection."

That stopped him cold. "One in a thousand?" The implications were incomprehensible. "One in a *thousand*?"

He could no longer bear to stand still and took off at a run up First Ave. Esmy followed him. They went over 20 blocks without seeing anyone else. Except for the wildlife, which had already reclaimed the place for their own, everything was still. There were no buses or cars racing by, no sounds of the subway emanating from under the pavement. Where before one could have heard a hundred different languages in a half hour's walk, there was silence. Some had found the city oppressive, unable to handle the endless tall buildings and thick density of people. For Daniel, it had felt, if not cozy, at least familiar and comfortable. It was this emptiness instead that threatened to overwhelm him.

At 42nd street, he stopped to stare at the flags of the world, still flying in front of the UN

Headquarters. "The Black Death killed a third of Europe in the Dark Ages. Measles and influenza killed 90 percent of the American Indians and toppled their greatest empires. What happens when 99.9 percent of the population dies?" he asked in a whisper. His back was to her, and the wind stole his words and blew them away, yet somehow Esmy still heard.

"That's only half of the question," she replied.

He turned around to look at her. Neither of them were winded by the mile and a half sprint, but Daniel didn't even notice. "What's the other half?"

"What happens when the surviving 0.1 percent becomes immortal?"

THREE

AS THEY CONTINUED TO WALK, she told him what she knew, which wasn't much. It was a disease unlike anything seen before: highly contagious, spreading by air and fluids, and showing no symptoms until the "sleep." By the time anyone had begun to notice something was wrong, it had already spread everywhere, quietly infecting untold numbers. The amount of patients soon overwhelmed the medical establishment's abilities to take care of all of them, and millions died of simple dehydration or starvation. Those who were kept alive became riddled with cancerous tumors, often dying within a few weeks. Quarantines were declared but too late. Seemingly overnight, digital communications around the world were lost, but most hardly cared. People were in a frenzy to escape doom, while many simply gave up on life and exposed themselves, lying down to sleep with their loved ones.

But there were survivors. Withstanding dehydration and starvation, they woke to a new reality. It was a shock, of course, yet in the end they did what humans have always done after an epic disaster: band together and try to pick up the pieces. Civilization was gone, but the remnants were all around them, and much was still usable: cars still ran, of course, and there was plenty of gasoline and diesel to be found to fuel them. Food was plentiful in grocery stores, and you could simply walk into any house you wanted and take what you needed. Resources meant for a million people now went to a mere thousand.

"So, anarchy?" Daniel asked. "Every man and woman for themselves?"

"There were a few who wanted that, and they ended up leaving and disappeared. No, we stick together, do our best to figure out how we're going to keep living. Nobody's officially in charge—we just do what we're capable of. Welcome to the tribe."

They turned a corner, and in Central Park, Daniel saw more people than he'd seen since he woke up. There were dozens milling around, a few children playing. "Do you know…is my uncle alive?" A part of him knew how stupid a question this was, but he couldn't help asking.

"If there were someone, I'd have taken you to them already. People always check the sleepers for loved ones, friends, even acquaintances. But no one knew you. I'm sorry."

Daniel had to sit down. He was not unfamiliar with death. His parents had passed away a long time ago, when he was very young. But this…

"He raised me," he said. "After the accident, when my parents were gone, he took me in. He taught me everything." Daniel couldn't continue. He broke down in sobs.

"Are you alright?" Esmy asked.

"I—I'll be fine," Daniel insisted through his tears. "It's just…how do you deal with it? You seem so collected, as if it doesn't bother you at all. Didn't you lose someone?"

Her face contorted briefly in some indescribable emotion, before settling on calm again. "I don't talk about the past, I don't think about the past. My old life is dead, and the old me is dead with it. That said, we all lost someone. You are not alone in this. They will help you. You'll be alright." Daniel nodded. "Are you ready to meet them?" she asked.

He drew a deep breath. "I guess so," he said. Esmy offered him her hand and helped him up again. "This is where we all live now, around Central Park," she said, her tone light and sensitive. "A few still stay wherever they did before, but I don't recommend it. It's just too lonely. In fact, most people have room-mates now too."

As far as he could tell, he was the oldest by a

decent margin; everyone looked under 25. The prevailing emotion wasn't fear, sadness, or despair—simple curiosity about the newest member of the community outweighed most other emotions. He was swarmed with friendly introductions and questions. A group of children found Daniel's bottomless stomach to be quite amusing and made a game out of providing him with a steady stream of whatever food could be found. So far, Daniel hadn't refused anything, or even slowed down. The whole situation was bewildering, but he couldn't resist the infectious good cheer.

A tall, muscular woman in a police uniform approached with a man in a gray hoodie and jeans. "Daniel," Esmy said, gesturing first to the woman in uniform then the man in the hoodie. "This is Siobhan and Hoang. Hoang you already met, if you remember."

"Think you'll manage to stay awake this time?" Hoang said with a wink. "You know, usually a man finishes before passing out on me."

"I, uh, yeah. Nice to meet you," said Daniel.

Siobhan rolled her eyes at Hoang. "Is this the skeleton you two were betting on?" She guffawed, then addressed Daniel. "Daniel, heh? Are you from the city?"

"Well, I moved here a few years ago. I'm not really a native—"

Siobhan waved Daniel's protestations away. "That doesn't matter. I just want to know how familiar you are with the place, or if you got trapped in the city like some idiots." She gave Hoang a pointed look, which Hoang studiously ignored. "What was your occupation before the sleep?" she asked.

"I teach…I mean, taught at City College. Biology."

Siobhan rubbed her chin. "Hmm. Not much work for a scientist these days. Got any other skills? Carpentry? Farming? Hell, even a musician could be useful. Gotta keep up morale."

"I…no, not really. I wasn't very interested in those sorts of things."

"Eh," Hoang shrugged. "It's fine. You can be useless like me. I was a software engineer. Not like Siobhan over here. Retired military turned police sergeant and a DIY hobbyist on the side…she's so practical it's almost disgusting. But hey, she'll figure something out that you can fake like you know what you're doing."

Siobhan snorted. "This is serious. We can't keep living off of what's just lying around," she said. "It's not going to last forever. We have to get self-reli-ant, growing our own food." She turned back to Daniel. "Well, in the new world, you're more or less unskilled, but that's okay. Human labor is back to being a main source of power, so there'll be more than enough for you to do. Hmm. What about guns? Have you ever had any training?"

"Well, it *is* New York. I didn't own any." Siobhan looked crestfallen and nodded in understanding. "But," Daniel continued modestly, "I did spend my weekends at the range."

"Oh?" said Siobhan, perking up. "The range? Well that's better than nothing. You'll need more training, of course, but that shouldn't take long."

"He's recovering pretty quickly," Esmy said, "but he was under for a longer time than anyone else as far as we can tell. He was down to his skin and bones. Besides, he's still in shock. Give him a little longer to eat and adjust before putting him on the barricades."

A voice crackled over a radio at Siobhan's hip. "Shots fired at the Willis Avenue Bridge, large force approaching, need backup."

"Roger that, Willis Ave," replied Siobhan, speaking into the radio. "We're on our way." She jerked her head at Hoang, who sighed and drew a pair of surprisingly large handguns out of his pants, what looked to Daniel like Desert Eagle 10-inch .44 Magnums. The two took off at a run to the north.

"Just wait here for now," Esmy said, turning to follow. "We'll be back soon."

FOUR

DANIEL KNEW THAT HE should probably listen to
her, but he couldn't stand the idea of being left
behind by the only person he knew. He followed
them at a distance up to 125th Street. As they
got closer, he heard what sounded like a pitched
fight. He started to feel worried, but the prospect
of walking alone all the way back to the others in
Central Park filled him with even more anxiety
than a shoot-out. Siobhan and Hoang continued

on 125th to First Avenue, where there was a make-shift barrier of Dumpsters and sandbags, manned by a small group of defenders. Esmy peeled off and went up the overpass that crossed just before the bridge. Daniel hurried to catch up with her. On the bridge, he could see a motley of SUVs, Jeeps, and trucks, with strange shapes huddled behind them, firing on their defensive positions. He looked closer and realized the shooters were all wearing bulky suits, like the kind he'd seen in pictures of doctors treating Ebola victims.

"What the hell are you *doing* here?" Esmy hissed as she saw him.

"I don't know," he said. "I just didn't want to be alone."

"You're not ready for this, get *down*."

No sooner had she said that when it felt like he was hit by a hammer, knocking him flat on his back. Looking down, he realized he'd been shot in the shoulder. "Stay down, you'll be alright!" Esmy shouted at him. Unlocking a gunbox that lay nearby, she pulled out a rifle and started shooting over the traffic barrier.

"Come and get me, you bastards!" she screamed. Daniel just lay dazed on the asphalt, wondering what the hell was going on, while the snow fell on his face and the sounds of battle raged around him.

Eventually it was all over. The gunfire grew more sporadic, then ceased. He heard engines rev and fade away. Esmy helped him to his feet. He had never been shot before, but he felt remarkably… fine. The wound ached a little, but had stopped bleeding a long time ago. Even more surprising was how calm he felt. They rejoined the others and began walking back to Central Park.

"What *was* that? Is everything okay?" he asked.

"A little foray by our neighbors," Siobhan said. "Nothing too serious, just needed proof that we weren't asleep on the job."

"Is it safe to be out? What if they come back?"

"We keep a sharp lookout on every entry to the

city," replied Esmy. "We'll know if they're back, and we'll fight them off again."

"Don't worry, Danny boy," said Siobhan, patting Daniel on the back. "Aside from the raids, there aren't many dangers to us now. The virus changes the survivors somehow. We don't get sick, we don't age, we can tolerate extreme conditions, and we heal," she gestured at his shoulder. "Well, like how you're healing right now."

"That's why we all look so young," Hoang said. "Fountain of youth flowing through our veins. I'm 36. Hell, Siobhan has to be at least in her 50s. She served 20 years before even joining the police! Now look at that fabulous skin. Not a single wrinkle." He reached out to caress Siobhan's face, but she slapped him, then punched him in the stomach. Hoang doubled over, though with pain or laughter, Daniel wasn't sure.

"But...how?" he asked.

"Who knows?" Siobhan replied. "Some claim it was divine intervention, or just the vagaries of pathology. Others blame the Russians, or the

Chinese, or the Muslims, or our own old government. But, whatever the cause, something must have changed our genes somehow. You're a biologist, right? Your guess as to the why and how is probably better than anyone else's."

"We probably have some jellyfish in us now, the kind that lives forever," interjected Hoang, who had finally recovered enough to stand up again.

Daniel snorted, but Hoang protested, "I'm serious. You'll see what I mean when it gets dark."

"Yeah," said Siobhan. "For once, he's not joking. All of us, we glow slightly in the dark. In fact, it's the first sign that a sleeper is going to survive and wake up."

"Pretty sweet, right?" said Hoang. "I'm not gonna say it's paradise, but it ain't bad being immortal. Really, just don't do anything stupid like jump off a skyscraper, and stay in the city, and you'll be fine."

"That, and find cover next time the uninfected come knocking," Esmy added.

"Wait, there are some people who didn't get

infected?" Daniel demanded.

"Yup," Hoang said. "No-glows. That's who just attacked us. You know, a few who somehow managed to avoid exposure."

"No…glow?"

"We glow, they don't. No-glow," Hoang explained.

"As far as we can tell, there are still way more of them than us," Siobhan said. "Luckily, most won't come into the city. Too afraid of contamination. We're all carriers for the virus, after all."

"Has anyone tried talking to them?"

"Of course we tried," said Siobhan. "One of the first things we did was set up a repeating radio broadcast, offering a truce, and saying that we just wanted to be left alone, but we've never gotten any response, other than more attacks."

Daniel shrugged. "Okay, they have guns, but we're immortal, right?" He fingered the hole in his shirt where the bullet had pierced it.

"Look, Danny boy," Siobhan interjected, "you can recover from just about anything that doesn't kill you right off, but a shot to the head is just as deadly to you as it is to a no-glow."

"It took a few failed attempts for the more sui-cidally oriented members of the tribe to figure that one out," Hoang said. "Slitting your wrists won't work, nor will most old-fashioned poisons. Heck, even hanging isn't a sure thing anymore."

Daniel shook his head. "I still don't understand why they would risk infection to attack us."

"Who knows?" Hoang said. "They're paranoid already. Anyone they aren't 100% sure is clean, they shoot on sight. And even when they're sure, they might shoot anyway, just to be safe. Maybe they think if they kill us all, the virus will just go away."

"It may have started as fear, but now it's hate," Esmy said, her voice grim. "They can't stand to think of how many of their loved ones died, so that a few of us can live forever. With nothing left to lose, they'll happily sacrifice themselves to kill us."

They continued walking in uncomfortable

silence for a while. With the sun well below the horizon and no electricity, the city was darker than Daniel had ever seen. "Holy shit," he exclaimed. In the moonlight, his hands and forearms glowed a soft blue.

"Like I told you," Hoang said smugly. "Jellyfish."

FIVE

WHILE RECOVERING FROM THE EFFECTS of not eating for half a year and getting shot, Daniel spent most of his time with Esmy. Hoang teased him for acting like a lost puppy, but Daniel drew strength from her firmly competent and reassuring presence. Unlike many of the others who spent their free time in idleness, she couldn't bear to sit still. She always had to be doing something, and in the new world, there was always something that needed to be done. They would collect food and store it centrally, move cars that blocked the streets; work in the hospital, treating the sleepers, or sometimes go to the library. Esmy agreed with Siobhan that they would need more skills in the community and spent long hours researching the old-fashioned, pre-internet way: with books. There were a few others who had a similar idea, and they would all discuss what they could do to thrive in their circumstances. Daniel had sat through a lot of bureaucratic meetings in his life, but these sessions were refreshing in their earnestness. There was no place for bickering and posturing now, only real solutions to real problems.

Following her advice, Daniel took a room in the same building as Siobhan and Hoang, and fell into a not-unpleasant routine. One night, Daniel dreamed of Esmy leaning over him in bed, like she had when he'd first woken up. She was smiling, and her long black hair fell over her shoulder to tickle his face. He smiled back. As he reached forward, she suddenly barked out, "Rise and shine, recruit!"

Daniel jerked awake to Siobhan's grinning, freckled face, just inches away. "It's 5 a.m., up and at 'em. You look healthy enough to me to start doing your duty, so let's *MOVE*."

She hustled him out of bed and into clothes, and led them out for a jog around the park. Daniel, in his previous life, had occasionally resolved to start jogging but always petered out after a single mile and a half loop around the Jackie O reservoir. Now he found himself moving at an easy lope for the six miles around the whole park. When they got back to where they'd started, his heart rate wasn't even elevated. He'd always hated exercise, but that was before he'd woken up with the endurance of an Olympic athlete.

"Good," said Siobhan, as they cruised to a halt. "Doesn't look like fitness is going to be an issue. Okay, let's see what you can do with a gun." They went to a low field surrounded by hills, which had been roped off and turned into an improvised range. Siobhan unlocked a gun box and gave Daniel his pick. There were a few 9mm pistols, a shotgun, and even a Colt M4 carbine, but Daniel immediately grabbed the rifle, a Remington 700P.

"Now, I don't know what kind of .22 peashooter you were using at the range before," Siobhan started, "but this is a real…" She stopped herself as Daniel loaded and then drew the rifle. Sighting a target at a hundred yards, he calmly hit the target three times, with one bull's-eye. Siobhan clapped him on the shoulder. "Boy, am I glad to have at least *one* person I don't have to start from scratch with."

Daniel blushed a little. "Well, I've only ever used rifles. I wouldn't trust myself with a handgun or anything else."

Siobhan shook her head. "Don't worry about that. We can give you all the training you could ever want in everything else, but for now at least, you'll make a decent sniper."

"I've never shot at anything living before though. I'm not sure if I could kill someone."

"There may come a point where it's us or them, and you should get used to the idea. We're not looking for a fight, but we're not going to apologize for living and roll over dead just to suit them either. Come on, let's get you a look at one of the barricades. Hopefully it'll go a little more smoothly this time."

Siobhan chose the George Washington Bridge. She explained that it was one of the least active barricades. Stretching over the Hudson, it was much longer than the Harlem River bridges that were more popular points of attack. Its length meant that approaching enemies could be sighted and fired on from a greater distance. The bridge had two levels, each of which was blocked off with abandoned vehicles. Siobhan was saluted by the others at watch. "Afraid of heights?" she asked. Daniel shook his head. She ushered him up the ladder in the suspension tower to a makeshift crow's nest. A few rifles hung nearby, along with ammunition and food, and other items. The weapons here were military grade. Daniel could only guess as to how Siobhan had gotten them.

The view over the river was pretty good. Daniel grabbed a pair of binoculars and looked at New Jersey. Things looked more like what he'd expected from the end of the world. Signs of looting abounded, and many of the buildings were burned-out husks. Guessing his thoughts, Siobhan explained.

"People fled the city early, not bothering to bring anything extra with them, and the first survivors to wake up quickly figured out not to make a mess for themselves. On the other side though…" she spat over the side. "The damn no-glows are just barbarians. Killing because they can, burning because it's fun."

As Daniel watched, a caravan of SUVs was coming down the Turnpike, headed to the bridge. "Uh, is that normal?" he asked, pointing.

"Yup," she replied, shoving a massive rifle in his hands and grabbing a carbine for herself. "It's a bit more than eleven hundred meters to the other suspension tower, so I'm going to wait till they're about halfway across the bridge before opening fire. You can fire at will though." Reaching for her radio, she said, "This is Siobhan at the GWB. We've got hostiles incoming at full speed. ETA under a minute. Fire at my command."

"Roger wilco," crackled the reply. Siobhan made a disgusted noise. "I keep trying to tell them that's redundant," she complained to Daniel, "but Hollywood buries things deep I guess."

"This is a Barrett Light Fifty," Daniel said. "I've never even seen one in person before."

Siobhan just shrugged. "You'll be fine. I'll spot you if you'd like. Here, use some ear protection. Your hearing will come back regardless, but trust me, it still hurts when you lose it."

Daniel swallowed nervously but accepted the earplugs and put them in. Siobhan did the same and waited patiently, lying on her belly, watching carefully through binoculars. He crawled down next to her, loaded the gun, turned the safety off, and sighted down the lane most of the caravan was traveling in. Breathing slowly and deeply, he focused on the cars as targets, not carrying people. It was just like a game. His finger rested lightly on the trigger. The cars were approaching the other tower. Breath in, breath out, pull. The gun bucked, and a hole appeared in the driver's side of the front windshield. The car swerved, crashing into another car, leading to a pileup.

Siobhan whistled. The attackers slowly pulled

themselves apart, returning to the western side without another shot fired. The SUV Daniel had hit didn't move. "Talk about seven at one blow," she said admiringly. "Damn. A bull's-eye on a fast-moving target at a thousand meters? I mean, you got lucky, of course, but luck alone isn't enough for something like that. Damn. Glad you woke up and joined us, Danny boy."

Daniel was shaking and sweating profusely as realization caught up with him. He had just killed someone, for the first time in his life. Someone he hadn't even seen. Adrenaline rushed through his veins, and he leaned over the side to empty his stomach. He wiped his mouth and fell flat on his back. Siobhan sat down next to him. Her jubilance softened, and she gathered him up in her arms.

"It's okay, Daniel. You did good. It's never easy to kill, but they'd have done the same to any of us, given half a chance. Shh, it's okay." She stroked his hair and hummed soothingly, and rocked him as he shook.

SIX

THE NEXT DAY, Daniel was still processing the events at the bridge. Word spread quickly in the tiny community about Daniel's shot (Siobhan magnanimously did not tell anyone about his subsequent breakdown), and he became the man of the hour. He was uncomfortable with the accolades, so he left Central Park and began to wander the streets, lost in thought. After a while, he found himself back at his old apartment building, by chance or subconscious desire, he wasn't sure.

Daniel hadn't returned since waking up. A wave of nostalgia came over him, and he fished out his keys to enter. He knew Esmy would disapprove, but he couldn't resist. Without a working elevator, he groaned out of habit at the idea of climbing to the fourth floor. He had always hated taking the stairs, but when he reached the end, he wasn't at all winded. He made his way down the windowless hallway to his apartment. It took him a few tries in the dark, but he finally got the right key into the dead bolt, turned it, and went in.

Everything was as he had left it. Even his suitcase was still by the door. He had no idea who had brought him to the hospital, but clearly they'd left his apartment alone. It was surreal. He sat down on the couch, in the same spot where he'd fallen asleep, and closed his eyes. It was so easy to believe that when he opened them, he would be waking up from that nap and everything would be normal. No supervirus, no apocalypse, just the routine of modern life. He opened his eyes and looked at his hands. They glowed faintly in the dark, and he let out a long breath.

Daniel stood back up and looked around to see

whether there was anything useful to salvage. He packed his suitcase with clothes and a backpack with food, and decided to leave the rest. He was about to go, when a letter caught his eye. Something about it tickled his memory, though he couldn't summon any recollection of it. Feeling the same overwhelming curiosity, he went over and grabbed it, folding it to put it in his pocket. With that, he closed the door and returned to Central Park.

———————————

"Where were *you*?" Hoang asked, when Daniel arrived at their stoop.

"I just went to get some things from my old place."

"Don't tell Esmy about that—you know how she disapproves."

"Yeah, I know. She's probably right. It did feel weird the whole time."

"Uh-huh," Hoang nodded in sage agreement. "Well, find anything good at least?"

"Just some clothes and food."

"Bo-ring."

"What can I say, I used to lead a pretty boring life."

Daniel smiled.

Hoang snorted. "I don't doubt it."

"What about you?"

"Me?"

"Yeah, what did you do before, well, this?" Daniel asked. He was genuinely curious. The only one of his new friends who had opened up at all was Siobhan, and she just talked about guns and tactics.

"Honestly," Hoang started, hesitating, "I was pretty boring too. I worked 16-hour days in front of a computer, thinking the whole time that I was solving real problems, that the things I was programming were going to make the world better. Hah! One lousy superbug, and everything I ever worked for is gone." Hoang had a dark expression on his face. "Do I miss it? I dunno, man, maybe. I feel like everything before the sleep was a lie, and now I've woken up, in more ways than one. But being awake is scary. We're all scared, even Esmy. She may try and act like she doesn't care about the past, but that's because in her case, it was *worse* before the virus. She won't say what exactly, but it must have been pretty bad if getting shot at every day, scrounging for food in the midst of your dead civilization, and not knowing a single goddamn person when you wake up is an improvement. The only one who really seems to be comfortable is Siobhan," he continued. "And that's because she's just doing what she always did: protecting people, serving the community, whatever. The rest of us really are just zombies. Walking around without a real clue as to what we're gonna do about anything."

Daniel didn't know what to say, so he sat down next to Hoang and gave him a hug. Hoang hugged him back. "Hey, man, I'm sorry, I didn't mean to get you down," Hoang said.

"It's okay," Daniel said. "You're not the only one thinking these things."

"I got carried away. It really isn't *so* bad. It's just like camping, I guess. Except in a dead city. And I never used to go camping, actually. But I'll adapt. I'll be fine. I may not have fixed the world in my old life, but I'll sure as hell do my best to make a difference in this one."

"I know you will," Daniel said.

Hoang, lost in thought, didn't respond. Daniel patted his friend on the back and continued to his room.

Putting everything away, he felt a crinkle of paper in his pocket and pulled out the letter. He sat down on the end of his bed and began to read.

DANIEL,

IT'S UNCLE JEFF. I'M WRITING YOU BY SNAIL MAIL BECAUSE IT SEEMS LIKE EVERYTHING ELSE THESE DAYS IS MONITORED. IT'S EXTREMELY IMPORTANT THAT YOU COME TO MY HOUSE AS SOON AS POSSIBLE. DON'T CALL ME. DON'T TELL ANYONE YOU'RE SEEING ME, JUST GET INTO THE CAR, RIGHT NOW, AND COME. THERE'S GOING TO BE A VIRAL EPIDEMIC AND I WANT TO KEEP YOU SAFE.

JEFF

Daniel's eyes went wide, and he ran out the door and into the street.

"Hey! Where are you going?" Hoang shouted.

"I need to talk to Esmy and Siobhan!" Daniel yelled back.

Hoang shrugged and followed at a trot.

SEVEN

"WHAT DO YOU MEAN, you need to leave the city? To see your uncle in New Jersey? Are you crazy?" Esmy asked. "He's probably dead by now anyway. Didn't I tell you to bury the past? This is a *terrible* idea."

"Esmy, this letter is postmarked *June 7*. You yourself said that I was one of the earliest cases you'd heard of, but somehow he knew about the outbreak weeks before that. He said he could keep me safe. If he could keep me safe, he's probably alive still too."

"Even so," said Esmy, "there's no guarantee that he could have avoided infection."

"And even if he stayed uninfected, there's a decent chance he got shot by someone," Siobhan added.

Daniel knew he didn't dare explain how much he yearned to see anyone from his old life, much less his uncle, who had been like a father to him. "Maybe, but he was a well-known geneticist. He had connections to all sorts of secret government and private biotech labs. If anyone would know something about this disease, he would. Don't you want to know why this is all happening?" he asked instead. "Where this thing came from, and what it's doing to us? We're driving blindfolded right now—what if he could tell us something important?"

Siobhan turned away, and Esmy made a disgusted noise in her throat, but Hoang laid his hand on Daniel's shoulder. "I think he's right," he said. "It could be worth investigating."

"It just seems like a stupid risk," Siobhan said.

"I don't know." Daniel shrugged, feeling very tired all of a sudden. "You're probably right. But I have to go."

"I'll go with you," Hoang said.

"Thank you," replied Daniel, "but—"

"I'll go too," Siobhan said abruptly.

"I thought you said it was a stupid risk," Hoang said.

"Yeah, it is," Siobhan replied. "Most likely we'll just find a blackened shell, Uncle Owen and Aunt Beru–style. But if you're hell-bent on going…there are too few of us survivors already to lose more. You'll need protection."

"Well it's a good thing I volunteered then," Hoang said to Daniel. "After all, who's going to protect you from *her*?" he jerked his thumb at Siobhan. "Have you ever heard her jokes? They're *terrible*."

"Stupid as you are," Siobhan said, "I'll still protect you too. When the no-glows come shooting, you'll all be glad to have someone who really knows how to shoot back."

"I don't think I can ask you to—" Daniel started, but Esmy interrupted.

"You're not asking. We're telling you," she said. "We're all four of us going. If this is what it takes to put Daniel's ghosts to rest, then we shall do it."

"It's not that—" he protested, but Esmy gave him a knowing look. Daniel looked at his three friends, whom he had met less than a week ago but who were already prepared to put their lives on the line to help him investigate a hunch. He swallowed the lump in his throat and nodded. "Thank you," was all he could manage to say.

"Fine," said Esmy. "But four is the max. We can't risk taking anyone else away from the defenses. Now, what the hell are we going to drive to New Jersey?"

"Don't worry," Siobhan said, with a sly smile. "I've got just the thing."

"A tank?" Hoang asked, his face expressionless.

"It's not a tank," Siobhan said. "It's a BearCat G3, an armored personnel carrier. Armor that can take a .50 cal round on top of a Ford F-550 Super Duty Chassis with a 6.7-liter Turbo Diesel, and…"

Daniel ignored the rest. He'd never been into cars, though he did have to admit that the thing looked pretty impressive. "Why not, Hoang? Looks like what we need for heading into hostile territory."

"I know," he muttered. "I just…I used to protest

against local police getting military-grade equipment. I never in my wildest dreams thought I'd ever be *riding* in one of these."

"Did you ever think you'd be an undying survivor of a cataclysmic disease?" Daniel asked.

"Touché," Hoang admitted. Siobhan kept up her enraptured monologue the whole time, blithely unaware she'd lost her audience.

"I know we no longer care about the environment," interrupted Hoang, "but this monster can't have much of a range, and I don't think we should be stopping for gas."

"I already told you, the gas tank is *huge*. We can get there and back easily. Also, with its high ground clearance, we can…"

Daniel tuned her out again. Loading his gear into the back, he hopped in. Esmy soon followed, with Hoang and Siobhan still bickering as they got into the front seats.

"Okay, the most direct route will be over the George Washington Bridge," Esmy said. "Plus, we probably have the best chance of punching through there. They can't be expecting us, and if this thing is as capable as you claim…"

Siobhan just patted the wheel and grinned. "Through or over, it's all the same to this beast."

———————

Even before the virus hit, New Yorkers didn't drive very often, given the cost and difficulty of driving oneself in the city, combined with the easy availability of the subway and cabs. Of course, neither of those were now options, but the traffic was gone too. In the beginning, as the survivors just began to wake up, they would often drive down the empty streets in expensive cars claimed for the day, but as the population became more concentrated around the southwest side of Central Park, there was little need to drive and the novelty quickly wore off.

Thus they found themselves the only vehicle on Broadway as they drove north. Siobhan had radioed ahead to clear a route, and the guards waved casually as they drove past the barriers.

"There's a place here, next to the bridge, the Little

Red Lighthouse," said Hoang.

Daniel nodded. He'd been by it before the sleep.

"I always wanted to have a picnic there and watch the sunset," Hoang continued. "I heard it was a pretty place on the river."

"It's within sniper range of Jersey," said Siobhan.

"That'd be a pretty good sniper," said Esmy.

"Don't worry," whispered Daniel loudly enough for it to be clear he wasn't seriously intending to speak privately. "We can go when we get back."

"It's a date then," grinned Hoang, with a wink. "You bring the food, I'll bring the bulletproof jackets."

"Cut the chatter. We're coming in," growled Siobhan. "Last call for seat belts—looks like you're gonna need 'em!"

They had opted to take the upper level of the bridge. They were sure to be spotted, but the lower level was much easier to seal off. The last thing anyone wanted was to be trapped in a tunnel. Esmy was proven right; the no-glows hadn't built much of a barricade. The wall was improvised from cars and not very sturdy—certainly not strong enough to withstand a nine-ton hunk of metal flying right at it at 80 miles per hour.

A few of the more foolhardy souls squeezed off a couple of shots from behind the barricade, but the rest just fled. Daniel steeled himself for impact, as with a whoop, Siobhan crashed through the cars. A few more shots were fired, some scoring hits, but the rounds bounced harmlessly off the armor before they sped away down the Turnpike, driving into the night.

EIGHT

"THAT WAS ACTUALLY PRETTY AWESOME," said Hoang.

"That's what I'm saying!" cried Siobhan. "Whoo! okay, now, give me directions, Danny boy. I don't know where I'm going."

For the first time since waking up, and even for a while before the coma, Daniel was happy. It had felt like he'd been shuffling through life without any direction, but now he was actually doing something, even though he had no idea whether they'd have any success. Besides, it had been so long since he'd had any sort of regular companionship.

The feeling was tempered by the destruction they found in New Jersey. The end of civilization had obviously left its mark on the city, but the changes were much more violent on the other side of the river. The survivors weren't the only ones subject to the constant threat of attack—there were signs everywhere of gunfights and other violence. He hardly recognized much of what he saw. None of this helped Daniel navigate. He hadn't driven in years, and when he had, it was always with GPS directions. It was even more difficult in the dark, and they took a few wrong turns, but with nobody else on the road, it wasn't hard to backtrack when necessary.

Finally, they reached a familiar tree-lined driveway. The gate was battered down, and the metal squealed underneath their wheels when they drove over it. None of his uncle's cars were in the driveway, and the house looked distinctly abandoned.

"Shit," said Siobhan.

"Doesn't seem like anyone's home," said Esmy.

Daniel had a sinking feeling. "Let me out. I'm gonna go take a look."

"One sec," said Siobhan. She parked the BearCat and came to the back, rummaging in a seat. She pulled out a SWAT ballistic jacket and helmet. "Here, just in case," she said, handing him the items. The other three also put on protective gear and, led by Daniel, exited the vehicle.

He tried the front door, but it was locked. He couldn't make out much through the front windows, but he thought he heard something.

"Someone's inside," he said to his companions and then banged on the door.

"Uncle Jeff!" he shouted. "Are you there?"

"Shush!" Esmy hissed. "You don't know for sure if whoever that is is your uncle!"

"Don't move!" a voice cried out. "I don't know what you're doing here, but leave, before I shoot!"

"Uncle Jeff?" Daniel yelled back, raising his hands in the air. "Is that you? It's me, Daniel!"

"Daniel?" his uncle replied, standing up from a second-story balcony to the side of the front door. "You're alive?"

"Yes! It's me."

"My God. Come, come in. Your friends too."

"Daniel," Hoang whispered, "he's not a survivor. He still looks *old*."

"Uncle Jeff, we're all from the city. We're carriers for the virus. I don't want to infect you."

"Wait, you *survived*? So then, you're biologically immortal! My God, there is some justice at least."

"Just stay up there, Uncle Jeff. We can talk this way."

"Alright, alright. After you didn't come, I thought for sure you were dead. It is so good to see you. I can barely…well. Your friends? Introduce me, Daniel."

After Daniel gave everyone's name, he said, "I'm sorry, Uncle Jeff—I swear I came as soon as I could. I didn't read your letter until after I woke up."

"Better late than never, of course. Damn post office probably delivered it late. Hah! Well, there's a problem nobody has anymore at least. No more post office, no more DMV, no more stupid HOA… always look on the bright side, right?"

"Uncle Jeff, I have to ask: how did you know about the virus? Your letter was postmarked weeks before most people got exposed."

Jeff's voice grew grim. "I'll tell you. For the past few years, I was working for a biotech start-up, GenomeTech. They had enormous funding. It was the worst-kept secret that they were backed by tech billionaires obsessed with escaping death. I finally had the resources to make real progress on creating transgenic humans, who would have boosted immune systems, cells that could revert to a juvenile state and regenerate, extending their lifetime indefinitely, protecting them from radiation and other environmental stress, and so on."

"Wait, transgenic? With genes from other species?" Hoang interrupted. "From jellyfish, right?"

Jeff nodded. Hoang hooted. "I *knew* it! That's why we glow."

"Actually, I have no idea why you

exhibit bioluminescence. We extracted genes from *Turritopsis dohrnii* jellyfish, which don't glow—also from lobsters, planarian flatworms, tardigrades, among many others."

"What I'm hearing is jellyfish and water bears," Hoang said. "Jelly bears. No! Gummy bears. We're gummy bears now, guys."

Siobhan elbowed him hard in the ribs as Jeff harrumphed. "Can it, dummy," she said.

"Sorry for the interruption, Uncle Jeff," Daniel apologized. "Please go on."

"At first, they just gave me anything I needed to do my own research in an open-ended grant, but they started to pressure me more and more. It turned out that George Polanski, one of the principal investors, was diagnosed with pancreatic cancer and was demanding results as soon as possible.

"His scientists demanded that I return to methods I had ruled out as too risky to deliver the genetic modifications. The difficulty was that everything needed to be balanced perfectly, otherwise the immortal cells would run amok as cancer. Using a virus as the vector was the only way I had achieved any success cases, but they were rare—about one in a thousand.

"One day, as I went into the lab, I discovered that a few vials of the virus specimen were missing. It didn't take long to realize what had happened: Polanski's goons had stolen it, to administer it to the old fool.

"Well, as you can imagine, it didn't work. He fell asleep and the cancer spread rapidly. They needed a scapegoat, so they blamed me for his death. I was fired, but I had already backed up all my data and hidden it.

"What I hadn't accounted for was the highly contagious nature of the virus. It spread and spread, but nobody other than me could recognize the symptoms, and nobody would listen to me. GenomeTech did everything they could to discredit me, not wanting to be held liable for an epidemic. By the time the broader public had any idea of the seriousness of the disease, it was too late to act. I quarantined myself in my lab, working desperately on a vaccine, cure, treatment, *anything*…and watched everyone die. I knew there were still some uninfected, but stuck out here with everyone shooting first and not sticking around to ask questions, I couldn't…"

A loud explosion cut him off, followed by gunfire.

NINE

THE BEARCAT BURST INTO FLAMES, lighting the darkness, and Esmy fell in a spray of blood. Daniel swore, grabbing her and slinging her over his shoulder with a strength he'd never had before. He followed the other two behind a low brick wall for cover. "Stay inside and get down, old man," Siobhan yelled over the tumult, before turning to fire back over the wall, joined by Hoang with his deafening pistols. Jeff followed her command, running inside and slamming the door shut.

"I'm okay, I'm okay," said Esmy, as Daniel laid her down. "It's just my leg. I'll be fine. Help them."

"Just your leg? Your leg is practically *gone*!" Daniel said.

"I'm not going to die! *Help them*." Despite her reassurances, she looked faint with the loss of blood, but there was nothing more he could do for her.

Daniel drew his rifle and loaded it. At first he couldn't make out their attackers, who were shooting from beyond the tree line, but he caught a glimpse of muzzle flash. Without thinking, he fired. A scream followed soon after, and for a time, there was quiet. Moments later, however, the assault began anew. Daniel shot back occasionally, trying to be judicious with ammunition, but eventually he ran out.

"Damn!" Siobhan swore. "I've never seen anything like this from them. This is my fault. I should have known they would throw more at us. We're on their turf."

"They can't allow us to think that we can ever escape," said Esmy. "They think they have to wipe us out now."

"So what do we do?" asked Daniel. "I'm out of ammo."

"Here, take my gun," said Esmy. "There are three rounds already loaded." She laid back and closed her eyes, fighting the pain.

"I've got two more clips," said Hoang, his face tight.

Siobhan swore some more. Their attackers had ceased fire, so she stuck the gun over the wall and fired at random until the magazine was empty. The immediate response was a hail of bullets. Siobhan loaded another magazine. "This is my last too," she said.

"Okay, listen up," Siobhan shouted over the noise. "They're not going anywhere, and obviously, neither are we."

"But, the BearCat, it's just singed!" Daniel protested.

"We can't make it to the BearCat! If we're going to get out of this, we've gotta take them out with what we have. They outnumber us and outgun us, but from what I've seen, none of them have any real combat experience, and I don't think they have the firepower to really smoke us out. They could wait, but I suspect they won't, and that impatience is our only chance. We let them think we're out of ammunition, then when they leave their cover, on my command, we hit them with everything we've got. After that, we can only hope."

They had few other options, none of them good, so they all nodded agreement. After a short time, the onslaught ceased. Siobhan cupped her hands and shouted, "Hey! We surrender! We're out of ammo, and we just want to go home!" More shots, for a longer time than before. The four of them covered their ears until it was done and then waited. They strained every sense in anticipation. Daniel and Siobhan peeked over the wall. The fires on the BearCat had died out, and in the dim starlight, they made out shapes stepping out of the trees and approaching the house, people in bulky hazmat suits.

"Hey! Hey!" Siobhan yelled again. "Surrender?" The silent shapes froze, but after a signal by one, started moving again. Daniel counted twelve. They were fanned out, but not by much. Siobhan signaled for him to take the three on the right, while Hoang would target those on the left, who were more bunched up. She would take the center and pick off any stragglers. The seconds seemed to take forever, as Daniel waited for Siobhan's signal. When the attackers were about twenty feet away, Siobhan yelled, "Now!"

The three of them crouched at the wall. Daniel fired once, twice, three times, each shot dropping a different target. Siobhan was firing in a steady, controlled manner, taking out attackers one by one. Hoang went berserk, screaming wildly as he unloaded his clips. Caught in the overwhelming firepower by surprise, the attacking force disintegrated. A few dropped all pretense of stealth and charged, firing blindly, while others threw their weapons away and fled. In a matter of seconds, nearly all twelve were cut down.

"Daniel!" shouted Hoang, springing in front of him. "Watch out for—"

The report of a rifle cut him off, as his face

exploded in gore. "No!" screamed Daniel. Hoang toppled over the wall. His friend's head was half gone. "Shit!" cried Siobhan. "You motherfuckers!" She shot at the last attackers, emptying her magazine into them, before dropping her gun to jump over to Hoang's body. "Goddamnit, you stupid idiot, you can't die—I said I'd protect you," she choked the words out between sobs. As she was dragging him back around the wall, another shot rang out, piercing her vest and taking her in the abdomen.

TEN

TOO LATE, Daniel saw one last gunman, on his side with a gun aimed right at Siobhan. She tried to raise herself but was shot again, this time in the shoulder. She crumpled, and Daniel leaped over the wall to shield her with his own body. Another bang, and his torso erupted in pain. He held her tight in his arms, eyes squeezed shut as he anticipated the end, but it didn't come. He rolled over and saw the gunman on his back, trying to clear his jammed gun. Ignoring the wound in his side, he hobbled over and wrestled the gun away. The man was frantic, scooting away on his behind, blood from multiple gunshot wounds pooling around him. Overcome with rage at the death of his friends, Daniel ripped the man's helmet off, prepared to tear his throat out with his bare hands if necessary.

"Stay away from me, you infected freak!" the man cried. Daniel fell to his knees, sitting on the man's chest, and hit him. He hit him again and again. Under his bloody fists the man shrieked, until a blow knocked him unconscious.

He heard his uncle cry out. "Daniel! Stop!" Jeff said. "This isn't you!"

"He killed Hoang and Siobhan!" Daniel wailed. "I'll kill him, I'll kill him!"

He raised his fist, but Jeff grabbed it. "You already have," he said. Daniel looked down at his blood mixed with the other man's, uninfected no longer.

Jeff helped Daniel up, before Daniel drew back in alarm. "Uncle Jeff, what are you doing out here? You'll be infected!"

"I know," said Jeff.

"But you'll most likely die!" Daniel broke down crying. "After all this, after…"

"Daniel, I was overjoyed when you came to me, when I thought I would never see you again. But then I had to watch you almost die, and I realized that I didn't want to spend my remaining days huddled alone in fear in this old house. I'm going to go with you, to the city. Besides, I didn't manage to finish. I've been able to develop a treatment that I think will improve survivability of the infected. I don't have any way to test it for sure, but it seems to work about half the time."

This news got his attention. "You…you have a treatment?" Daniel asked.

"Yes!" Jeff said. "It took months and it's not perfect, but it's better than nothing."

Daniel was still shaking his head, but there was nothing else that could be done. "Come on, Daniel," said Jeff. "Let's see to your friends, and then if you don't mind, I could use a hand loading some equipment into your tank."

"It's not a tank," croaked Siobhan.

On the banks of the Hudson near the Little Red Lighthouse, Daniel and Siobhan buried Hoang, while Esmy sat in a wheelchair nearby. When they finished, Daniel planted a small headstone, bearing the inscription:

Nguyen Hoang
GUMMY BEAR

"I'll miss that fool," said Siobhan, sniffling.

"He was a better man than he'd ever admit," said Esmy.

"He died for me," Daniel said. "He saved me. I can't—I shouldn't have…"

"And you will honor his sacrifice," Esmy interrupted firmly, "by living the life he would have wanted for you."

She wheeled herself to him and held his hand, and Siobhan embraced them both. They watched the sun set over the river together. Just before twilight, a bullet zipped by and buried itself in the ground a few feet away. The three scrambled for cover in the old BearCat, abandoning the wheelchair as Daniel carried Esmy inside. Siobhan laughed as they drove away. "I told him that was a terrible spot for a picnic!"

"One hostile gang down, who knows how many left to go," Esmy said.

"Don't worry," Siobhan said. "We'll make it through. We're survivors."

Siobhan dropped Daniel off at the hospital, where Jeff now lay unconscious in the same bed Daniel had occupied. His uncle had fallen asleep soon after arriving to the city, but he had had enough time to give the treatment and instructions to Daniel. It took regular doses, and Daniel never missed a course. Every night, he entered his uncle's room, hoping to find the telltale luminescence that announced that Jeff would wake up and dreading to see the cancerous lumps of the unfortunate souls who could not successfully incorporate the new genes. But like all the previous nights, there was no change yet this time. Daniel administered the medicine through the IV and sat down next to the bed. Picking up his uncle's limp hand, he held it, until exhaustion overcame him.

As he slept, his uncle's hand began to glow faintly.

THE END

ACKNOWLEDGMENTS

For such a small book, I got a lot of help.

First and foremost, I have to thank Eliot Peper. There was no stage, from inspiration to brainstorming to writing to editing to publishing, in which Eliot did not play a critical role. He is a true friend, and a magnificent creative spirit.

Jesse Vernon did an excellent job editing the prose, catching the kinds of errors that would have been an endless source of embarrassment if published. Kenny Sheftel ensured that important details were as plausible as possible. Chris Saavedra read every single draft and was a key creative partner, helping me to make many important decisions. My own Uncle Mark contributed Uncle Jeff's handwritten letter. Kevin Barrett Kane of The Frontispiece designed the entire book, outside and inside, and it is no exaggeration to say that he is a genius.

My mother raised me, educated me, and always supported my writing ambitions, starting with the very first book we produced when I was four years old, *Side-Kings and Robin Hoods*.

There is no room to acknowledge all the authors whose books have been transformative experiences, but without their stories, I couldn't have told mine.

Finally, thank you, dear reader, for letting me into your head for a time.

ABOUT THE AUTHOR

NICK FARMER is a writer and linguist based in Oakland, CA. He created the Belter conlang for Syfy's *The Expanse*, contributed to the best-selling introductory linguistics textbook published by MIT Press, and works to support endangered and indigenous languages. When he's not writing, he loves spending time outdoors, lifting weights, listening to music, puttering around in his mess of a garden, and watching baseball.

To find out more, visit his website (www.nickfarmer linguist.com). You can stay in touch via his author newsletter, Facebook (www.facebook.com/nickfar merlinguist), and Twitter (@nfarmerlinguist).

Made in the USA
Lexington, KY
21 April 2017